-ed as in bed

Amanda Rondeau

Consulting Editor Monica Marx, M.A./Reading Specialist

Published by SandCastle™, an imprint of ABDO Publishing Company, 4940 Viking Drive, Edina, Minnesota 55435.

Printed in the United States.

Credits
Edited by: Pam Price
Curriculum Coordinator: Nancy Tuminelly
Cover and Interior Design and Production: Mighty Media
Photo Credits: Digital Vision, Hemera, Donna Day/ImageState, PhotoDisc

Library of Congress Cataloging-in-Publication Data

Rondeau, Amanda, 1974-
    -Ed as in bed / Amanda Rondeau.
       p. cm. -- (Word families. Set II)
       Summary: Introduces, in brief text and illustrations, the use of the letter combination "ed" in such words as "bed," "shed," "red," and "sled."
       ISBN 1-59197-228-0
       1. Readers (Primary) [1. Vocabulary. 2. Reading.] I. Title. II. Series.

PE1119 .R69 2003
428.1--dc21

2002038627

SandCastle™ books are created by a professional team of educators, reading specialists, and content developers around five essential components that include phonemic awareness, phonics, vocabulary, text comprehension, and fluency. All books are written, reviewed, and leveled for guided reading, early intervention reading, and Accelerated Reader® programs and designed for use in shared, guided, and independent reading and writing activities to support a balanced approach to literacy instruction.

Let Us Know

After reading the book, SandCastle would like you to tell us your stories about reading. What is your favorite page? Was there something hard that you needed help with? Share the ups and downs of learning to read. We want to hear from you! To get posted on the ABDO Publishing Company Web site, send us e-mail at:

sandcastle@abdopub.com

SandCastle Level: Beginning

-ed Words

bed

fed

led

red

shed

sled

Ned is sleeping in his bed.

Ann fed the goat.

Bill led his friends.

Beth's team wears red shirts and caps.

We keep tools in the
shed.

The Smith family went
down the hill on a sled.

Ed Is Too Tall for His Bed

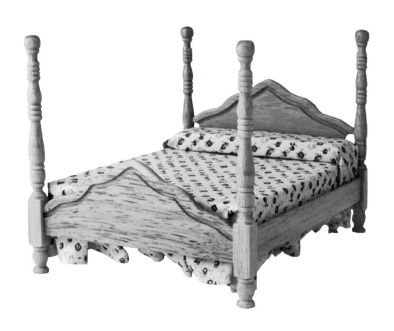

There
once
was a boy
named
Ed.

Ed was very tall.
His dad kept
him well fed.

Ed had grown
too tall for his bed.

15

16

He told his
problem
to his
brother Ted.

"I grew too tall, too,
and I know what
to do," said Ted.

Ted led Ed
to the shed.

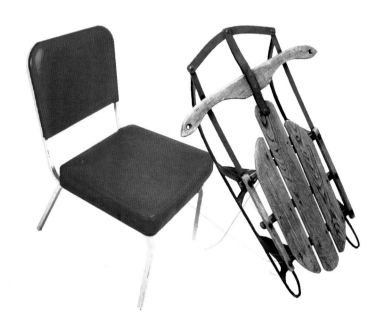

Next to a sled,
they found a chair
that was red.

And they set it at the
end of the bed!

The -ed Word Family

bed	shed
Ed	shred
fed	sled
fled	sped
led	Ted
Ned	wed
red	

Glossary

Some of the words in this list may have more
than one meaning. The meaning listed here
reflects the way the word is used in the book.

down   toward the ground or
            bottom

found   past tense of find; to
            discover accidentally or as
            the result of seeking

goat   a mammal with horns that
            is often raised on farms for
            its milk

problem   a situation that needs a
            solution or thought

shirt   a piece of clothing for the
            top part of the body

tool   a device you use to help
            you do a chore

About SandCastle™

A professional team of educators, reading specialists, and content developers created the SandCastle™ series to support young readers as they develop reading skills and strategies and increase their general knowledge. The SandCastle™ series has four levels that correspond to early literacy development in young children. The levels are provided to help teachers and parents select the appropriate books for young readers.

Emerging Readers
(no flags)

Beginning Readers
(1 flag)

Transitional Readers
(2 flags)

Fluent Readers
(3 flags)

These levels are meant only as a guide. All levels are subject to change.

To see a complete list of SandCastle™ books and other nonfiction titles from ABDO Publishing Company, visit www.abdopub.com or contact us at:

4940 Viking Drive, Edina, Minnesota 55435 • 1-800-800-1312 • fax: 1-952-831-1632